Tawny Pa-Pawny and the Late Late School Bus
(Book #2)

Written and Illustrated By T. P. McKinnon

Contents

Copyright Info

This is a work of fiction.

Tawny Pa-Pawny and the Late Late School Bus Book #2

Copyright © 2012 by T. P. McKinnon

ISBN 9 781105 600074

Hi my name is Tawny Lynn Brown. My mom's name is Tamara and my dad's name is Randy. I am six years old. I have a big brother named Sam and a pet turtle named Duke. We all live in a big house in the middle of our street. The "bestest one," I said. We have lots of fun at our house. Today Jessie is too sick to come to school. So Momma said I can catch the bus all by myself.

CHAPTER ONE

"All By Myself"

I told Momma that I would be okay. Jeez, it's only at the corner. I can still see the house from the bus stop. I thought to myself as I finished pinning a pink rose barrette in my hair.

"Tawny you better get a move on before you're

late for your bus!"

"Alright Momma, I'll be right down."

I put Duke back in his bowl and reached under my bed to look for my book bag. Not there, but what a mess. I quickly dusted off my skirt and hurried downstairs to find my mother standing at the bottom of the stairs with my lunch in one hand and my book bag in the other. I looked down to make sure my shoelaces were tied.

"Okay Momma I'm ready."

I grabbed my book bag and my lunch and stood on my tippy toes and kissed her goodbye.

"Don't forget keep your eyes peeled for strangers."

"Momma I can't peel my eyes, but I will be careful and make sure I get to school on time."

"Okay honey, I hope you have a great day."

"By Momma love you!"

"Love you too dear!"

I quickly ran down the steps and started to skip past the houses on my street. No one was outside this morning. Jessie was lucky that he got to stay home. The sun was shining so bright and the flowers in Jessie's yard were beginning to bloom. I stopped at the stop sign at the corner. Alright this is it. The bus stop for Bus # 22. I turned around and saw Momma peeking out the front door and when I looked across the street, Jessie's mother was outside picking up some paper in the front yard. I let out a sigh and leaned back against the gate. The bus should be coming any minute now, I thought. Jessie and I catch the same bus every morning at 8:15 a.m., Bus # 22. I think Momma said that it was 8:05 when I left.

I looked down on the ground and saw all the gum that was stuck on the sidewalk. A lot of gum eaters catch the bus. I found a piece that was sticking up from the ground and began to push it back and forth with my sneaker until it rolled up into a little ball. It was hard and sticky. Eww! I reached back and pulled my book bag down off my shoulders and found a clean spot in the grass to sit it down.

Maybe we'll get Ms. Morris as the bus driver today. She is hilarious. She's tells us stories on the trip to school. She says she used to work in the circus as a clown. I just thought her nose was red cause she had a cold. I leaned forward and looked down the street. The bus was nowhere in sight. I went and stood near the curb and looked down the street again and this time

I could see all the way down to Ms. Clark's house and still no bus.

The sound of two girls giggling came from around the corner. One of them was in the bigger grade at my school. I don't know her name. I just see her in school a lot. She's nice. She always smiles at me. I turned to look as they walked by and she looked at me and smiled and said

"Hi, my name is Susie and this is my friend Kim we are in the 4th grade. Haven't I seen you around school before?" "Why are you out here by yourself? Did you wake up late this morning?"

"No my friend Jessie is sick today so I had to catch the bus all by myself cause

Momma said it was okay.
Momma told me to keep
my eyes peeled. The bus
seems to be lost or
something."

"Well that's probably
because you missed it. I
know because we catch
the bus after you and you
are never at the bus stop
when we catch it. So
that means you must be
late."

"I hope not, I don't want

to miss school. The bus
has to be on time. I have
a math test today."

"Well we gotta go Tawny.
It was nice to finally get
your name and all. Too
bad you can't catch the
bus with the bigger kids.
We'll see you in school I
hope, she said with a
giggle."

I waved goodbye to them
both as they walked
down the block. I

stomped my foot as I looked up into the sky and spun around and around in a circle. The wind was blowing a little bit. As I stopped spinning I reached to grab onto the fence so that I wouldn't fall over. Woo, I stood still and when I looked up I saw that Momma was now standing on the front porch. I smiled and waved.

She yelled "no bus"?!
I shrugged my shoulders
and said nope. "It must
be the late late bus."

"Tawny honey there is no
late late bus!" She
started to walk down
towards me at the bus
stop. "Well, I guess you
don't have to wait by
yourself now."

CHAPTER TWO

"Momma's Baby"

"Momma, you can't stand here with me, everybody will call me a baby."

"Oh Tawny don't be silly, no one would think that."

"Yuh huh!" My friend Cameron stood at the bus stop by himself one day and he forgot his hat.

His Momma came to give him his baseball cap, just as two of his friends from school was walking by and when he made it to school that morning everybody was saying "Momma's baby."

"Well how about if you walk way in front of me and I walk way behind you til we get home. Will that be okay?"

"Gee thanks Momma, that would be great. Then I'll still look like a big girl."

"Okay, let's get going so you won't be late for school."

"Okay Momma." I turned and reached for my book bag and lunch bag, which were sitting in the grass behind me. I get to ride to school with Momma in her car. Maybe she'll

even let me sit up front.
Who cares about that
stupid late late bus
anyway?

"Alright, Tawny are you
ready?"

"I sure am Momma."

"Okay then start
walking."

I turned and made my
way back home. This was
going to be great. I

skipped past all of houses that were before my house. Boy were they pretty. Only thing is I thought our house was the bestest one, because the porch was big enough so that everybody could sit down at one time even Duke.

Just as I bent down to tie my shoelace, I heard a sound coming from down the street. It sounded like it could be my school bus. I jumped up and yelled "Momma, Momma the bus is coming! The bus!"

Momma stopped and pointed and said, "Look." It was a little blue car that came speeding around the corner. It was so loud it sounded like a school bus.

"Oh well, let's go inside. I'll call your teacher and tell her you're gonna be a little late and I'll make sure everything is locked up before we go."

"Momma, can I sit on the porch?"

"You sure can, but stay on the porch." I dropped my things and sat down with my chin resting in my hands. I couldn't believe it. The first time I catch the bus by myself and I miss it.

CHAPTER THREE

"The Late Late School Bus"

I stared down at the sidewalk and noticed my old hop scotch board was still there from the other day and Duke's little rubber ball was in the grass right where I left it. I turned my head sideways and what do you know. Coming down the

street. Just as late as it
could be the late late
bus.

I knew there was one.
I stood up on the porch
and put my hands on my
hips. My face was now in
a frown.

"Well, what do you know.
Momma the late late bus
just went by! If only I
waited at the bus stop."

She came to the door

and said "Tawny, what are yelling for, young lady?" I looked at her and pointed down the street.

"Well, I'll be a monkey's Aunt. The late late bus."

"Yeah, I know."

"Well no use frowning over spilled milk. I called your school and they know you are going to be a little late. The class hasn't started yet anyway. So what do you say about us taking the long way to school? Since we missed the late late bus. I'll even let you ride in the front seat."

"Wow! Momma can I open the window just a little bit?"

"Of course, but not for too long I don't want you to catch cold."

Momma locked the door and went to the garage to lift up the door. I ran into the garage and opened the car door to put my bags in the back seat and I climbed into the front seat. Momma started up the car and we slowly moved out the garage and into the street. Momma hit a button in the car and the door went back down.

"Hey, how'd you do that?"

She looked at me and gave me a wink.

"Do you have on your seat belt?"

"Yes, I do Momma."

"Alright lets go. We'll make it just in time for your class to begin. Who needs to ride the late late bus anyway?"

"Not me." I let my hand hang out the window and felt the cool morning air on my face.

"Not me Momma!"

THE END

Giggle more with Tawny Pa-Pawny and Friends!

TURTLE FACTS:

*The oldest turtle fossil found was dated back
230 million years ago during the Triassic Period.*